Magic Runs Wild

(A Novel for Teenagers)

Kaitlyn Nguyen

Ukiyoto Publishing

All global publishing rights are held by

Ukiyoto Publishing

Published in 2024

Content Copyright © Kaitlyn Nguyen

ISBN 9789364941228

All rights reserved.

No part of this publication may be reproduced, transmitted, or stored in a retrieval system, in any form by any means, electronic, mechanical, photocopying, recording or otherwise, without the prior permission of the publisher.

The moral rights of the author have been asserted.

This is a work of fiction. Names, characters, businesses, places, events, locales, and incidents are either the products of the author's imagination or used in a fictitious manner. Any resemblance to actual persons, living or dead, or actual events is purely coincidental.

This book is sold subject to the condition that it shall not by way of trade or otherwise, be lent, resold, hired out or otherwise circulated, without the publisher's prior consent, in any form of binding or cover other than that in which it is published.

www.ukiyoto.com

Contents

One	1
Two	11
Three	23
Four	32
Five	38
Six	47
Seven	54
Eight	60
Nine	66
Ten	73
Eleven	77
Twelve	82
About the Author	*92*

One

"So," my best friend, Isadora whispered, leaning in conspiratorially, "did you hear about Beatrice and what happened to the love potion?"

My eyes widened. "No way! Tell me everything!"

Isadora chuckled, her voice barely above a murmur. "Apparently, she was trying to impress this older student from the Water Magic division, what's-his-face... Finn?"

"Right, the one with the unfairly chiseled jawline," I supplied, a grin tugging at my lips.

"Exactly! Anyway," Isadora continued, her voice dropping to an even lower whisper, "Beatrice somehow messed up the recipe, and poor Finn ended up uncontrollably attracted to... Headmistress Marietta's prized bonsai collection!"

I burst into a fit of stifled giggles, imagining the stoic Headmistress chasing a lovesick Finn around the greenhouse. "Oh my stars, that's hilarious! But what happened next?"

Isadora shrugged. "No one knows for sure. Rumor has it Professor Hawthorn used some advanced calming spell, and Beatrice is currently banned from the Potions lab for a month."

I looked around the Grand Hall to see the nervous faces of the freshmen reflected on the polished stone floor. A kaleidoscope of colors danced across the room, courtesy of the ornate stained-glass windows. Each color represented a different Elemental Division– orange for Fire Magic, blue for Water Magic, a vibrant green for Nature, a bright yellow for Light Magic, violet for Dark Magic, and cyan for Ice Magic. Each person possesses an inherent connection to a specific element. This connection defines our **Elemental Division**, shaping the type of magic we're most adept at wielding.

Ugh, when is it going to begin? My stomach did a nervous flip-flop.

Hi, I'm Lysandra Gleason, I'm 11 years old and a fairy about to attend Asteria Institute , the most prestigious school for fairy Magic in all of North America! If you wondered what the exams to get into Asteria are like, well, picture a three-part gauntlet that tests your magical core and your personality under pressure that will determine which Elemental Division you're going to be in. Part one was deceptively simple, all you had to do was channel your innate magical energy on your open palms. Mine tingled with a warm light. Each examiner had to carefully examine each student and take notes on the characteristics of the energy produced, based on the heat, color, and intensity. Remember Isadora? Her magic crackled like summer lightning.

Next up was the written exam, which Professor Priestley, a stern woman with round spectacles perpetually perched on her nose, assured us that it wasn't going to be your typical exam. No, this was an exam with personality and scenario-based multiple choice questions designed to expose your magical tendencies. Here's a sneak peak: You discover it's about to rain heavily while enjoying a picnic. **What do you do?**

A) Pull out your umbrella.

B) Gather things speedily.

C) Try to will the clouds away.

D) Laugh it off as an amusing surprise.

E) Make swift movements to gather things.

F) Consider creating an icy shelter.

The final hurdle was the interview, it was….less of an interrogation and more of a friendly chat. The heavy oak door creaked open to reveal a sight that instantly calmed nerves. An upperclassman, named Penelope, with her fiery red hair a stark contrast to the cool emerald of her robes, stood on the other side. The interview with Penelope wasn't what I expected. Her energy was wild, and the room smelled like dirt and spices. But she was funny, and her take on the questions actually made sense. I felt a lot less nervous after talking to her!

"So, did Penelope give you any hints about your element?" Isadora whispered, her eyes sparkling with curiosity

I shrugged, the nervous feeling from earlier returning. "Not really. She was all over the place, talking about gnomes and calming scents. Though, she did say the written exam wasn't as bad as I thought."

A sly smile tugged at my lips. "Well, she did mention something about how some questions test your instincts, like calming a grumpy gnome with... wait for it... the right scent!" I winked at Isadora. "Maybe I aced the calming part." Isadora's eyes widened. "Calming scents? You think you might be..." Her voice dropped to a conspiratorial whisper, "Light magic?"

Suddenly, a booming voice echoed through the Grand Hall, "Freshmen! Please form a single line and proceed to the Hall for the Ceremony!", said Headmistress Marietta This is it, it is time to find out which division I'm going to be in! A hush fell over the Grand Hall as the first freshman placed their hand on the pulsating crystal ball. The orb glowed a brilliant blue for a moment, then settled on a steady violet, announcing their placement in the Water Division. Everyone knew the drill. Each freshman would step forward, clasp the crystal ball, and the orb's magical reaction would reveal their elemental alignment. The color-coded glow was unmistakable: yellow for Light, violet for Dark, green for Nature, red or orange for Fire, blue for Water, and an ethereal cyan for the rare Ice magic.

The line snaked its way forward, with each student approaching the crystal ball at the center of the hall, anxious about what would be revealed. With every passing turn, my anxiety climbed another notch. I watched, my heart pounding, as Amelia Lovelock, a girl with fiery red hair tied up in a high ponytail , stepped forward. A moment later, a triumphant yell erupted from the Fire Division, followed by a burst of orange light from the crystal ball, Amelia was Fire Magic, no surprise there. Next up was Isadora. She stepped in front gracefully, almost gliding across the flagstones. Extending one hand, she hovered her palm over the pulsing crystal ball. I found myself holding my breath. The orb's rhythm seemed to slow as Isadora made contact. For a moment, it simply continued its steady thrum. Then, like a dawn breaking through the night sky, a warm golden light began emanating from within the crystal's depths. The radiant aura grew brighter and brighter until it encompassed the entire ball in a radiant sunny aura. A cheer erupted from the Light division. She gave me a subtle wink before gliding over to join her division. A pang of envy, quickly squashed by genuine joy, for Isadora, flickered through me. Now, all eyes were trained on me. It was my turn. What element would the crystal ball assign me? I smoothed my dress and took a deep breath before stepping forward. The warm glow still emanating from the orb after revealing Isadora's alignment seemed to beckon me closer. As I extended my hand, my fingers trembled ever so slightly. I watched with bated breath as the orb cycled through a kaleidoscope of colors - fiery oranges, deep forest greens, brilliant sunshine yellows. Finally, it coalesced into a steady, pale yellow aura enveloping the crystal ball.

"Lysandra Gleason", the Headmistress's voice was warm yet resolute, "you have been sorted into the Light Division". A wave of relief washed over me, quickly followed by elation and pride. Isadora was beaming from the Light section, giving me an enthusiastic double thumb's up. We were in the same division!

The sorting ceremony pushed onward at a feverish pace after Isadora and I joined the Light section. A slender boy with shaggy hair was up next - the crystal flared a brilliant verdant green to mark him as part of Nature. "Wyatt Caddel, Nature elemental division!" Headmistress Marietta called out over the murmurs. Wyatt didn't seem surprised, simply nodding stoically before joining the small cluster of green-clad students. As the next girl, Rebecca Palmer, approached the orb, I leaned over to Isadora. "What element do you think she'll be?" Before Isadora could respond, the crystal began glowing with a pulsing violet luminescence, dark as a raven's feathers taking flight at night. "Rebecca Palmer... Dark Magic division," came Headmistress Marietta's cry, drawing a few gasps. The slender brunette's expression remained blank as she drifted over to the section filled with others radiating that same aura of mysterious, spectral energy. Based on the reactions, I gathered Dark wasn't the most common elemental alignment. On and on it went, each new glow from the crystal eliciting hushed whispers and frenzied analysis. The burly, rough-looking guy who got sorted into Fire Magic? No shocker there based on the roar of approval from that section. But I don't think anyone anticipated the demure, rosy-cheeked girl being designated for Ice - her slight frame was instantly sheathed in sparkling, crystalline fractals as she shivered over to the smallest division. Finally, after what felt like an eternity, the ceremony had finally ended! As Headmistress Marietta called out the final division placement, she turned to address we newly-sorted students...

"Welcome to Asteria Institute. Today you have been sorted into your respective elemental divisions through our ancient ceremony. Whether you now call Light, Dark Magic, Nature, Fire, Water, or Ice your magical home - you all now share one critical distinction: you are now students of Asteria! As students, there are rules and codes of conduct that you have to abide by. First and foremost, the use of magic outside of supervised lessons is STRICTLY prohibited unless explicit permission is given by other professors. This is for your safety and the safety of others. Magic is a powerful force, and wielding it without proper training can lead to disastrous consequences. Now that you have been sorted, please proceed to the front desk in the main office to register and receive your official student identification card. This card grants you access to your dorms, the library, and other essential areas of the school!"

After the delicious start of the year banquet, I left the hall to go to the Front Desk at the Main Office. Pushing open the doors, I was met with a sight that clashed spectacularly with the ancient magic I'd felt moments ago. The once-austere Main Office was now a sugary explosion of pink and red. String lights in the shape of hearts twinkled overhead, casting a rosy glow on the room. Sentient teddy bears, their button eyes gleaming with an unsettling cheer, sat perched on every available surface. Even the stairs leading to the upper floor were adorned with helium-filled pink balloons, a precarious display that threatened to topple over at any moment.

"Ah! Lysandra!!!", Penelope exclaimed cheerfully, "You're my favorite interviewee this week! You're new here, aren't you? Let me get you an ID card!" I was surprised to see Penelope, "Pe-Penelope? What brings you here? Weren't you at the year-opening banquet?!" "Oh, I decided to volunteer here this semester!", Penelope offered with a light-hearted shrug. This intrigued me. "Volunteer?" I echoed, a bit taken aback. "But given your advanced studies and your earth magic expertise, wouldn't your time be better devoted to studying ancient incantations or something similar?"

Penelope laughed warmly. "Ah, Lysandra, magic isn't all about fancy spells and making potions. There's a charm, let's say, in keeping things tidy and organized." "So…are you ready to pick up your dorm key?", Penelope asked "Yeah!" , I responded

With that, Penelope bent down and started rummaging in her cabinet, With a triumphant "Aha!", Penelope emerged from her search, holding a shiny key. "Here you go, Lysandra! This is your key to the Light Division dorms. You know, you're really lucky you've got me today at the front desk, because I'll let you choose your favorite room, AND make special arrangements for you to live with any of your friends! Or, did I read you wrong? You can have the whole room to yourself!"

"Oh, by the way, I forgot to hand you this!", Penelope pushed a silver book into my hand, "This is a bewitched daily planner, the book magically updates itself with class schedules, homework reminders, and a to do list tailored for you! It can be opened to any date to view the day's scheduled activities, lessons and tasks. Notes and assignments added to the planner are automatically organized by class and priority, and helpful notifications and alerts keep you on track to avoid missed deadlines or forgetting to do homework!

"Actually, Penelope," I spoke up, excitement coloring my tone. "About those special arrangements you mentioned for rooming? I was hoping, if it's at all possible..." I glanced over at Isadora, who was waiting nearby. the door. "That you could room Isadora and me together? We're absolutely inseparable." Penelope's eyes twinkled merrily as she nodded. "But of course! I'd be delighted to make those arrangements for my two favorite interviewees. Let me just magically etch both your names onto this key..." She waved her wand and muttered an incantation. The key glowed briefly before returning to normal. "There we are, one dorm for Misses Gleason and Fairbourne in the Light Division dormitories," Penelope declared with a wink. "I may ..have also taken the small liberty of ensuring your room gets optimized with all the latest comforts!" Handing me the key and the newly minted student ID, Penelope shooed us away. "Now run along you two! I'm sure you're simply dying to get unpacked and catch up on all the gossip before classes start tomorrow!" My face lit up with unbridled glee as I rushed over to Isadora, holding up the key triumphantly. "Can you believe it? We get to be roomies!" Isadora laughed, throwing an arm around my shoulders as we headed out. "Of course I can! I don't think there was ever really any doubt, was there? Now come on, you know Beatrice will never let us live it down if someone else hears about the bonsai incident before we do..."

Two

Our classes next day were a blur of textbooks, bubbling cauldrons, and whispered spells. Professor Priestley's Charms class was as organized as her bun. Every textbook was precisely stacked, and not a single potion bottle was out of place. Her expression was as stern as a stone statue, with her round glasses perched on her nose, glinting like polished amber. Her class was as challenging as I expected, my wand feeling more limp than a cooked noodle when I attempted the Levitation Charm. Professor Cuthbert's Botany class wasn't in a classroom at all, but a giant greenhouse overflowing with the most enormous and incredible plants I had ever seen. Gigantic flowers bloomed in colors that would make a sunset jealous, and tiny leaves shimmered with an otherworldly glow. Even the air seemed different in here, buzzing with the soft whir of unseen fairies and the occasional chirp of a particularly chatty bird. Professor Cuthbert herself assured us that Botany wasn't nearly as scary as the rumors made it out to be. Thankfully, Professor Whitlock's Potionology class was next. His outfit was a riot of color, and it was stained with exotic hues, and his wild white eyebrows seemed to have a life of their own. Professor Whitlock's lessons were ANYTHING but dull — exploding cauldrons, bubbling potions, and the occasional whiff of something distinctly like burnt dragon scales. He even let us taste a laughter potion today, which turned poor Beatrice into a giggling mess for the rest of the afternoon! When the sweet melody of fluttering pixie wings signaled the end of Professor Whitlock's class. I practically leaped out of my seat, my head buzzing with a mix of excitement and exhaustion. I met Isadora by our usual spot at the Light Division section, and we tucked into our porridge.

"Professor Priestley is…strict," I admitted cautiously, as I ate my porridge

Isadora snorted, a mischievous glint in her eyes. "Strict? Try terrifying! I swear I saw a first-year levitate his quill by accident and then faint dead away from her stare."

I giggled. "Maybe a little dramatic, but I wouldn't want to disappoint her!" I paused, then added, "Professor Cuthbert's class, though? That was amazing! Did you see those flowers that smelled like blueberry muffins?"

Isadora's eyes widened. "You're kidding! I love Professor Cuthbert! She reminds me of my grandma – all warm smiles and endless cups of tea. But honestly, I had a blast in Professor Whitlock's Potionolgy class. Did you see the color-changing potion he made? It was like a miniature rainbow in a bottle!"

"Eh, Potionology seems….complicated. All those weird ingredients and all of that", I shuddered, "I'd rather stick to talking to plants, thank you very much".

Isadora nudged me playfully. "Don't be such a scaredy-cat! Professor Whitlock makes it fun. Besides, you never know what amazing things you can create with a little experimentation! "Well, to be fair, Professor Whitlock's class was chaotic, but definitely interesting", I admitted to Isadora.

After classes had ended that first exhilarating yet exhausting day, Isadora and I made our way back to the dorm Penelope had so generously arranged for us in the Light Division dormitories. As we were walking, I couldn't tear my eyes away from the beautiful fairy wings Isadora's family gifted me that had manifested along my back.

Isadora's family was a Noble, and they are part of an extremely prosperous lineage that specialized in producing exquisite fairy wings. From what I gathered, Noble lineages could be traced back further than most. Their ancestors played important founding roles and made noteworthy contributions over generations, which makes them one of the most prestigious families in the magical community. Not to mention the SIGNIFICANT amount of wealth they have.

While they considered me and my parents - who were professional healers- like family, it was clear they held Isadora to a higher standard when it came to being a Noble. "Can you blame them?" Isadora had said when I complimented the wings. "I may be an only child, but I'm their precious light fairy. They expect me to quite literally embody perfection. Also, I'm a Noble, my family is practically royalty. We simply don't do anything half-winged!"

My conversation with Isadora faded into the background as we approached the Light Division Department. Unlike the red-brick buildings I'd pictured, the Light Division Section was breathtaking. Glowing white stones formed the walls, curving organically into the landscape. Wispy vines with moonlight-colored blossoms climbed the structure, and butterflies with iridescent wings flitted between them.

A low hum emanated from the building, a melody that seemed to vibrate in the very air. I gasped, a soft sound escaping my lips. This wasn't like anything I'd ever seen.

Isadora, usually the picture of composure, couldn't help but let out a low whistle beside me. Even she seemed speechless.

A young woman with hair like spun gold and eyes that mirrored the light of the dorm walls emerged from the building. Her smile was as warm and welcoming as the first rays of dawn.

"Welcome, new students!" she chirped, her voice like wind chimes. "I'm Seraphine, your Resident Advisor for the Light magic dorms. Come on in, don't be shy! Your rooms are waiting for you."

Isadora and I exchanged a bewildered glance, then hesitantly followed Seraphine inside. The interior of the dorm was just as impressive as the exterior. Soft orbs illuminated the common room, casting a warm glow on the pale stone floor. Comfortable armchairs beckoned us to relax, and bookshelves overflowed with spellbooks promising forgotten lore. "Are you

Isadora Fairbourne and Lysandra Gleason? Please follow me! I'm going to guide you through your dorms!", Seraphine said. We followed, speechless. Inside, the dorm pulsed with a soft, inner light that bathed everything in a warm glow. The pale stone floor seemed to shimmer, and I couldn't help but stare, mesmerized. "Let's get you settled in. Your dorms were placed with a lot of charms for maximum comfort, but feel free to personalize them with your own magical flair. Just remember, no uncontrolled levitation experiments after midnight, see those little specks flitting around the chandeliers? Those are pixies. Just try not to wake them with any late-night spells, alright?"," Seraphine said.

Pixies. In my dorm room.

The dorm was a breathtaking sight, it was bathed in a gentle lavender glow. Vines with pale blue flowers climbed the walls, and a window offered a view of a shimmering waterfall cascading into a moonlit pool. Isadora's room, on the other hand, emanated a cool, silvery light. A large, star-shaped window dominated the back wall, and constellations swirled across the pale ceiling. There was an ornate wall motto emblazoned above the stone fireplace's mantel that captured my attention: "*Let your light shine bright, for even the smallest spark illuminates the darkness*" I squinted at the swirling script. "'Let your light shine bright, for even the smallest spark illuminates the darkness.' "Huh, deep stuff." Seraphine smiled warmly. "It's one of our core principles we try to instill. About using your inner light to dispel shadows and negativity, you know?" "Ooh, I feel so enlightened already," Isadora said sarcastically

I nudged her with my elbow. "Be nice! I kind of like the message. It's like...motivational but still pretty cool, you know?" Isadora rolled her eyes teasingly. "Leave it to a light fairy to find a glowing wall quote inspiring instead of lame." "Whatever, like you wouldn't get all starry-eyed over a cheesy astrology poem carved into the dorms," I shot back with a grin.

"What's with all the commotion here?" a voice chirped, brimming with enthusiasm. "Are we late for the welcoming party or something?" I turned around to see Cassidy Clarke, a first year from the Light Division.

A wave of amusement washed over Isadora. "Party? We were just being shown our rooms," she replied.

Seraphine, who had been watching the exchange with a warm smile, chuckled. "Ah, this must be Cassidy Clarke! You girls are dormmates!". Still a little overwhelmed, I managed a shy smile. "Lysandra. This is Isadora."

Seraphina gestured towards Cassidy. "Cassidy, you've been placed in Room 214 with Lysandra and Isadora. It seems fate has brought together three Light magic novices!"

"Epic, huh?" Isadora mused, a hint of amusement in her voice. "Yeah", I replied.

Cassidy, oblivious to the deeper conversation happening between Isadora and me, bounced on the balls of her feet. "Speaking of epic, my stomach's starting to rumble like a troll after a particularly large goat. We wouldn't want to miss any leftover pastries from dinner would we?"

Isadora sighed dramatically. "Food? Must you always think with your stomach, Cassidy?"

Cassidy grinned unfazed. "Someone's gotta make sure Asteria's food doesn't go to waste! Besides, you know I can't resist a good éclair."

A genuine smile crept across my face. "Alright, alright, lead the way, food connoisseur. But maybe on the way, you can fill us in on what we missed at the banquet yesterday." The idea of catching up on the festivities piqued my curiosity.

Cassidy's smile widened. "Oh, you bet I can! Get a load of this," she began, her eyes sparkling with excitement. "So, you know how every year at the opening banquet, all the representatives from the Asteria Student Committee give speeches, right?"

"Mhm," I nodded eagerly, leaning in to listen, feeling a surge of curiosity. "Well, let me tell you, this year's speeches were totally something else," Cassidy continued, her voice tinged with excitement, "We had the usual from the representatives; Anastacia Marigold from the Light Division, Keiran Blackwell from the Dark Magic Division, Floraline Windward from the Nature Division, Aiden Blaze from the Fire Division, Finn Harper from the Ice Division, and Marinne Pearson from the Water Division. But there was one moment that stole the show."

My interest was piqued. "What happened?" I asked, my eyes wide with anticipation.

Cassidy leaned in, lowering her voice conspiratorially. "You know Beatrice, the fifth-year girl who's head over heels for Finn from the Ice Division? Well, right in the middle of Finn's speech, she bursts in and confesses her feelings for him!"

I gasped softly, surprised by the boldness of Beatrice's actions. "Right in front of everyone?" I whispered, my heart pounding with excitement.

"Right in front of everyone," Cassidy confirmed with a mischievous grin. "It was like something straight out of a romance novel. Beatrice was practically in tears, pouring her heart out to Finn."

I couldn't help but feel a mixture of admiration and sympathy for Beatrice. "And how did Finn react?" I asked, eager to hear more.

Cassidy chuckled. "Well, Finn being the responsible Ice Magic representative that he is, he handled it like a pro. He thanked Beatrice for her honesty but told her they could talk later, after the ceremony."

I nodded thoughtfully, impressed by Finn's composure. "Wow, what a moment. I can't imagine how brave Beatrice must have felt."

"Yeah, she definitely took everyone by surprise," Cassidy agreed.

As Cassidy regaled us with tales from the banquet, we made our way through the corridors of Asteria. As we turned a corner, we nearly collided with Penelope, who seemed to be in a rush.

"Oh, sorry about that!" Penelope exclaimed, her voice cheerful despite the near collision. "Didn't see you there! Hey, Lysandra! Isadora! How are my favorite interviewees doing?"

"We're doing great, thanks!" I replied, offering Penelope a warm smile. "Just getting the grand tour from Cassidy here."

Penelope's eyes twinkled with amusement as she glanced at Cassidy. "Ah, Cassidy. Leading the newbies on another adventure, I see."

Cassidy grinned, her excitement palpable. "You know it! Just giving them the lowdown on all the gossip from the banquet."

Penelope chuckled. "Well, I'm sure they're in good hands with you, Cassidy. But don't keep them out too late, alright? We don't want any lost first-years wandering the halls."

"Don't worry, Penelope," Isadora chimed in, her voice light and playful. "We're in capable hands. Right, Cassidy?"

Cassidy straightened up, determination gleaming in her eyes. "Absolutely! No lost first-years on my watch."

Penelope laughed, her melodic laughter echoing through the corridor. "Alright, I trust you three. But if you do get lost, just give a shout. I'll come rescue you with my trusty map."

With that, Penelope waved goodbye and continued on her way, disappearing around a corner. As we watched her go, I couldn't help but feel a sense of gratitude for the warm welcome we had received from the upperclassman.

"It seemed like, when Penelope was saying 'Well, I'm sure they're in good hands with you, Cassidy. But don't keep them out too late, alright? We don't want any lost first-years wandering the halls,' Cassidy wasn't a first-year," I whispered to Isadora, barely able to contain my amusement.

Isadora stifled a laugh, her eyes sparkling with mirth. "Classic Penelope, always treating Cassidy like the seasoned pro she isn't."

Cassidy, unaware of the subtle irony, beamed at Penelope's words. "Did you hear that? Penelope trusts us to navigate these halls like seasoned veterans."

"Of course she does," Isadora replied with a playful grin. "Because we're practically experts at getting lost."

Cassidy's grin faltered for a moment before she joined in on the laughter. "Hey, who needs a map when you've got people like me?"

"Penelope's always so friendly," I remarked, turning to Isadora and Cassidy. "It's nice to know we have someone like her looking out for us."

Isadora nodded in agreement. "Definitely. And she's not just friendly, she's also super helpful. Remember how she hooked us up with our dorm arrangements?"

Cassidy grinned. "Oh yeah, Penelope's like the fairy godmother of Asteria. She's got connections everywhere."

As we walked into the Grand Dining Hall, the air was filled with delicious smells that made my stomach growl. The hall was a bustling hive of activity, with students from all six Elemental Divisions mingling and chatting over plates piled high with food.

At the Light Division table, where Isadora and I usually sat, fruits and vegetables in hues of gold and amber adorned the table, their vibrant colors glowing softly under the enchanted lights. Salads glistened with dewdrops, and pitchers overflowed with a refreshing, citrus infused drink that sparkled like liquid sunlight. Meanwhile, the Fire Division table was a fiery spectacle, with Amelia Lovelock, one of the most popular students in school, enthusiastically tucking into a plate of flamed grilled dragon meats and spicy peppers. Marinne Pearson, a representative of the Water Division, was eating a large salmon. Cassidy led us to grab some food, her eyes sparkling with excitement as she chatted about what we missed at the banquet.

The orb at the center of the hall emitted a soft, melodic tone, reverberating throughout the school, signaling the end of the day. With a collective yawn, we bid each other goodnight and headed back to our dorm rooms.

I had a strange vision that night.

Solaria howled, "Nyx, I understand the trials damaged your faith in humans, but we cannot judge all of them by the actions of a frenzied few!"

Nyx screamed back, "A few? I saw dozens tortured and killed for our kind's power, which they'll never possess! Their fear and hatred will always be just under the surface!" Solaria replied, "There IS fear on both sides born of misunderstanding, but with time and empathy, non magical folks and fairies will learn to coexist!"

"Coexist? Why bother, when we could end their threat entirely? You and the others coddle them at our expense! Have your lessons taught you nothing of how fleeting their trust can be?"

"Fighting hate with more hate will just make everything worse. We need to set a good example of accepting people different from us!", Solaria sighed dramatically. Nyx let out a screech, "Your "example" is what got witches slaughtered! From now on, fairies and humans go their separate ways. If you don't get it, then you're against me too!"

"No! Please Nyx, trust me! I'm not against you, I swear! Separating everyone won't make things better. Just hear me out - we can talk with each other find a peaceful solution if we work together instead of against each other."

"Talk? All you ever do is talk, Solaria! While you preach your nonsense, I saw my sisters burned! But what would perfect little Miss Sunbeam know of pain? You stay here with your textbooks while real fairies face the dangers outside!"

Solaria felt tears welling up at the cruelty in Nyx's voice. "Nyx, please...we're on the same side."

"The same side?" Nyx laughed mirthlessly. "All I see is a coward too afraid of her own shadow. Well I don't need your sympathy or your weak-willed tolerance!"

Three

The next morning brought a bright and cheery start to the day at Asteria Institute. I headed off to the classroom for our first lesson of the day: Basic Magical Theory.

As I stepped into the room, there was Professor Hatchett, looking all scholarly and serious at the front of the class. He had a crisp appearance and meticulous demeanor that gave off an extra aura of authority, like he knew everything there was to know about theoretical magic, though there was a hint of crankiness in his expression. With a nod of acknowledgment, he launched into the lesson.

Settling into my seat, I listened intently as Professor Hatchett explained how different types of magic could interact with one another, creating powerful effects when properly harnessed. But before long, the peace of the classroom was shattered by the arrival of Amelia Lovelock. She was confident, athletic, and undeniably popular, she was the epitome of everything I was not.

As I hurried to Astronomy class, hoping for a more peaceful environment, I couldn't shake the feeling of Amelia's presence lingering behind me like a shadow. When I arrived at class, I found myself face-to-face with Professor Laurier.

Taking my seat, I glanced around the room, noticing that Amelia had somehow managed to find her way into this class too. Great. Just what I needed. I offered her a small nod, hoping to diffuse any potential tension, but she responded with a haughty smirk that told me she wasn't about to let bygones be bygones.

As Professor Laurier began her lesson on celestial bodies and their influence on magical phenomena, I tried my best to focus. But with Amelia shooting me smug glances from across the room, it was easier said than done. Sure enough, as Professor Laurier launched into her lecture, I could feel Amelia's mocking gaze boring into me from across the room. Out of the corner of my eye, I noticed her leaning over to whisper something to her Fire Division friends, who all snickered in response.

Heat rose to my cheeks but I determinedly kept my eyes forward, scribbling notes on my notebook as Professor Laurier described the movement of celestial bodies. But it was hard to focus with Amelia and her friends giggling intermittently, as if sharing an inside joke at my expense.

Just then, a crumpled ball of paper sailed through the air and bounced off the back of my head. I turned, seeing Amelia smirk as she idly inspected her nails, playing innocent. My fists clenched under the table but I didn't dare give her the satisfaction of a reaction.

As Professor Laurier's lesson drew to a close, I began packing up my things, dreading what was next on the schedule – Flight. I heard Amelia whispering taunts to her friends again and steeled myself for what was to come. With trepidation, I made my way to the stadium for our first Flying lesson. Professor Swift, was a stern but fair witch, and was known to have won a lot of awards for competitive flying.

"Summon your wings and stretch them fully from root to tip," she demonstrated. I focused and felt the soft sensation of my wings appearing.

"Now perform some warm-up flaps," said Swift. "Flap strongly but smoothly up and down." I joined the rhythmic flapping, feeling my wings grow steadier.

"When ready, kick off into a hover," instructed Swift. With a leap, I pushed skyward and fought to maintain balance. Others soared circles around me with practiced control.

"Now glide between the trees," directed Swift, motioning lithely through the gaps herself. I wove unsteadily after her example as classmates flew in formation.

"Return and perform sprints across the glade on my mark," said Swift. At her whistle, I shot unevenly forward while Amelia and friends zipped in perfect sync. My wings felt weak, struggling to stay aloft. Laughter echoed from nearby as Amelia and her friends did loops around me effortlessly.

"Look at Gleason go, she flies like my gran with arthritis!" shouted Amelia, to howls of amusement from the others. My face burned as I tried to block them out, concentrating fiercely on not falling.

By some miracle, I made it through the lesson intact, if utterly humiliated. On the ground, Amelia sidled up with a sneer. "Quite a show up there, Gleason. Your flying was pathetic even by first-year standards."

I pushed on shakily under Professor Swift's instruction, trying to block them out. But Amelia wasn't done.

"Bet her wings are made of tissue paper! No wonder she can barely get off the ground," sneered Eliza, zooming loops around me.

Professor Swift called for us to glide between the trees, which I managed only clumsily bumping from trunk to trunk.

"Even the trees have more finesse than Gleason!" howled Madeline. "At least they don't flap around like dying bugs!"

By the time we reached the sprints, I was red-faced and faltering. "Look, she's running out of steam already!" cried Amelia. "I'd bet my wand Gleason couldn't last one full lap!"

Her friends shrieked with mirth as I battled onwards. But their insults took their toll - on the third lap my wings abruptly gave out and I plummeted.

"Pathetic!" laughed Amelia.

"Leave her alone, she didn't want all of that rotten behavior from you vultures," said Isadora boldly.

Amelia sneered. "Ooo, sticking up for the loser? Fairbourne, are we Noble?" she mocked. "And just what are you going to do about it?"

"Yeah, we all know Noble blood means nothing without power to back it!" cackled Eliza.

Isadora met Amelia's eyes steadily. "My heritage means nothing here. But I suggest taking your stupid insults elsewhere before a teacher intervenes."

As we walked back to the castle, I absentmindedly fingered the sunstone pendant Isadora gifted me around my neck, Isadora patted my shoulder reassuringly. "Don't let her get to you Lys! Come on, it's sunny outside - want to study in the courtyard?"

Her suggestion lifted my spirits. "That sounds perfect, thanks Iz"

We made our way across the field, the afternoon sun warming our wings. My mind turned from Amelia's threats to enjoying time with Isadora.

Isadora and I found a spot under the cherry blossoms. As my gaze drifted over the courtyard, I noticed once again the gleaming Fountain of Elysium at its center.

"Who created that fountain?" I asked Isadora. "Do you know its origins?"

She nodded. "It was crafted by Solaria, one of the original founders of Asteria. She imbued it with light magic to power the barrier hiding the school from non-magicals"

I stared at the fountain, awestruck. "So light fairies maintain it then? Keeping the enchantments strong after all this time?"

"Exactly. They sing charms and renew the protective spells daily," Isadora explained.

My eyes travelled up to the fountain's peak, where a small marble statue of a pixie with long twin tails gazed out serenely. "Is that meant to depict Solaria?" I questioned.

Isadora looked up. "Possibly. Though some believe it represents the first fairy entombed in stone who blessed the fountain with her magic."

Just then, a fairy emerged from the waters, her shimmering wings wet from the fountain. As if on cue, her voice carried on the breeze, weaving a new layer of magic into the charm. The shield over the school grew imperceptibly brighter.

As we greeted Cassidy when she walked into the courtyard, she looked me over with concerned eyes. "I heard that the pathetic douchebag Amelia bullied you ," she said. "People were talking about it in the corridors - seems she can't help but make a spectacle of herself."

I sighed dramatically, "I guess she just really loves the attention.."

Cassidy scoffed, "Of course she loves the attention. She only just arrived here but she's already the most popular student in our year, just because everyone fawns over her natural talent for flying and her good looks".

Isadora nodded understandingly. "It is true that Amelia is popular with many of our classmates. But who cares about that anyway?"

Our deep conversation by the creek really helped me feel better. Before long, dusk was falling and our stomachs started growling.

"I don't know about you two, but I could really go for a chicken salad from the dining hall," said Cassidy. We all laughed and made our way back up to the castle.

With full bellies from the Grand Hall, we decided to see if Penelope in the main office needed any help before turning in for the night.

As we entered, Penelope greeted us warmly from behind the front desk. "Thanks for stopping by girls, I could use an extra set of hands if you're willing!"

She walked us through answering calls on the orb line, welcoming the occasional late visitor, and helping organize records for staff. Penelope was always so busy supporting the whole school.

Before long, dusk deepened into night outside. "You both should get some rest," said Penelope with a smile. "But I really appreciate you lending a hand this evening. Now hurry along to your tower - goodnight!"

After helping Penelope, we made our way cheerfully back to the dorm. Stepping inside, Cassidy eagerly retrieved her Asteria Academy student planner.

"Let's see what's on tap for tomorrow!" She said with a grin. Our custom planners were magically tailored with suggested activities and schedules.

Cassidy read that spell practice duels and useful charms lessons were recommended to make us feel better. As we were dueling with each other, the room filled with sparkling bubbles, dancing shadow puppets, and other playful spells. We laughed so hard our sides hurt! Isadora then showed us handy charms for tidying our space - "You messies could use some cleaning help," she teased.

Isadora talked Cassidy through a tricky Charms essay, helping connect its concepts into a clear outline. I struggled with potions terminology, so Iz quizzed me on antidotes until I finally remembered them

With homework and daily tasks complete, we relaxed chatting happily until yawns overtook us. After that, we bid each other goodnight, and went to our rooms to sleep.

The sky was looking nasty as clouds rolled in. The tension between Solaria and Nyx was ramping up. One last time, Solaria pleaded desperately for them to talk it out. But Nyx was at the end of her rope.

"If you will not listen to reason, then you leave me no choice" she screeched. Shadowy tendrils snaked around her limbs as her anger manifested.

Solaria stayed glowing bright, hopeful it wasn't too late. "We're stronger together than apart. Our pain doesn't have to divide us!"

Lightning crackled from Nyx's hands. "Time for actions, not speeches!" She threw a bolt at Solaria.

Solaria blocked it, but the force sent her sliding. She gathered her warmth into fiery yellow balls, hovering in her palms. "You give me no choice."

Their magic was spiraling out of control, just like their fight.

Four

In the next few days, Asteria holds the annual Sports Championship. The anticipation around school has been building each day as we count down to the start of tryouts. Even in the corridors, heated debates break out at every turn regarding who stands the best chance of making the divisional teams. Even our professors seem caught up in placing friendly wagers!

As I watched Cassidy train fiercely from the sidelines in preparation for tryouts, I knew my own flying skills would never cut it for championship level competition. I remembered all too well my humiliating performance in Flying class and Amelia's relentless taunts. While I wished Cassie the best of luck, a part of me was also relieved not to have to face the pressure and risk of public failure myself. As Cassidy and I chatted before tryouts, Isadora walked over to join us. "So Cass, are you feeling ready for tryouts tomorrow? Me and Iz have been helping design some killer cheer routines to support our team." I asked. "I think so," Cassidy replied with a sigh. "But I'm still so nervous, the competition is going to be fierce! Did you see Amelia flying laps around the stadium today? I'll be happy just to make the team at this point.

"Don't sell yourself short, you've got a great chance," Isadora encouraged Cassidy. " Your speed is unmatched and gymnastics are stellar. Just remember to relax and have fun with it too!"

"Easy for you to say Iz!" Cassidy laughed nervously. "You're not the one who'll face campus-wide disappointment if I botch it."

"We'll be cheering you on no matter what," I assured her. "And even if you don't make the official team, you'll still be champion in our eyes."

Cassidy smiled at that. "Thanks Lys, that means a lot. I'm just praying I don't freeze up."

"You won't, you've come so far. And we'll be right there with pepper-up potions if you do!" said Isadora confidently.

By the end of our talk, Cassidy seemed slightly calmer. I hope she performs well in the tryouts next week.. Headmistress Marietta announced that the students that aren't participating won't be allowed to observe the tryouts in person. But Isadora had a secret weapon - she learned a complex invisibility spell which, if performed correctly, could conceal us both so we could watch anyway! Though at first, I was hesitant to break the rules, but my desire to support Cassidy overrode any doubts. As we walked into the stadium on the morning of the tryouts, Isadora turned to me with a determined glint in her eyes.

"It's time. Let's get into position."

We picked our way carefully through the shadows towards the stadium stands. Once there, Isadora withdrew her wand and her Charms and Spells textbook and began pacing, muttering to herself. "Occultum... no, too broad. Occultum viewers... hmm." Finally she stopped, squaring her shoulders. "I've got it. Stand close now." She took a deep breath and began a intricate figure-eight motion with her wand, chanting clearly: "Occultum!"

A shimmering veil seemed to descend around us, and everything took on a sparkling, hazy quality. Isadora smiled, "It worked! I can barely see us, how do you feel?" "Like I might dissipate into thin air at any moment," I admitted nervously. The magic felt highly unstable. Isadora nodded knowingly. "It'll hold long enough, but we'll need to concentrate to maintain it. Complex spells aren't my strong suit yet. Let's find a good vantage point before my strength fails!" Day 1 of the tryouts was Swimming. Sabrina Myrtle from Dark Magic and Marina Hampton excelled in the water. Cassidy shined too, outpacing Angelica from Light Magic in freestyle. Beatrice was too busy stealing covert looks at Finn to focus fully. Day 2 of tryouts was Fairy Gymnastics. Isadora and I met before tryouts, with our arms full with contraband popcorn from the kitchens. We enacted our spy routine to sneak into the stands under Isadora's concealment spell. Angelica, Hazel from Nature, and Cassidy were all performing ridiculously difficult routines on the bars and apparatuses. Cassidy's flexibility had the professors taking many notes. It was clear that she had a chance of making it on the Light Magic team.

Day 3 was Wing Sprint. The fairies took flight in a whirlwind of wings. Cassidy and Finn took an early lead as expected. But to our surprise, Beatrice seemed to have gained confidence - her wings were steadier and she had closed the gap on some of the other competitors! Cassidy and Finn pulled ahead quickly, neck and neck until the end. In the final moments Cassidy edged out a victory, with her and Finn as top contenders in the race.

Day 4 was Archery. Sabrina dominated the target practice. Cassidy proved steady with a bow as well, consistently hitting targets. Nature and Dark magic students led here, but she held her own.

Day 5 was Track and Field, and also the last day of the tryouts. Cassidy and Angelica battled fiercely, but Cassidy prevailed in the 100m sprint at the last moment. Sabrina and Hazel took home ribbons too. Beatrice tripped on her javelin throw.

With the tryouts now complete, it was clear the top contenders to make the championship teams included Cassidy, Finn, Sabrina, Angelica, Marina, and Hazel based on their performances throughout the week. But the official team selections were still to be announced on Monday.

During tryouts, the Dark Magic competitors tended to display cutthroat attitudes, in contrast to other divisions showing more sportsmanship. "Sabrina Myrtle was constantly elbowing other fairies out of the way during the races," Isadora noted. "And in archery, I saw Keiran Blackwell deliberately distract opponents to throw them off their shots. Not very sporting, huh?"

As Isadora and I made our hasty exit from the now-dissolving concealment spell, a familiar voice rang out.

"Well well, what do we have here?"

We froze in our tracks, exchanging an "uh-oh" look. Slowly, I turned to find Professor Broderick eyeing us with poorly-concealed amusement. Of course it would be one of the sports instructors to catch us sneaking from the stands!

"Fancy meeting the two of you here," he continued, cocking a brow. "Did you happen to be, should we say, watching without permission?"

Isadora summoned her most sincere expression, "I'm so sorry professor, we only wanted to support our friend Cassidy in the tryouts. We never meant to cause trouble, really!

Affecting my very best doe eyes, I chimed in. "Please don't tell Headmistress Marietta, we'll accept any punishment quietly." Professor Broderick chuckled, shaking his head. "I'll let it slide this time, but don't make a habit of it. Consider it a warning, I won't be so lenient if it happens next time." "Thank you so much Professor!", I answered.

Isadora and I made our way cheerily back towards the Light Division dormitories after our narrow escape from Professor Broderick. As we arrived at our dorm, we saw Cassidy sitting beside the fireplace, looking at us suspiciously. We slowed our approach as Cassidy asked pointedly, "And where have you two been off to in such a hurry?" "Oh you know, just hanging around," Iz replied airily. But Cassidy wasn't buying it.

"Cut the act. I heard from Angelica that Broderick caught a couple snoops at the stadium." She fixed us with a knowing look.

I sighed. "Ok fine, we may have tried to peek at tryouts..." Cassidy shook her head, but I could see the smile creeping through. I opened my mouth to explain but Cassidy raised a hand, silencing me with a very stern look. "Honestly you two, do you have any idea how concerned I was for you guys when I heard what you've done? Do you even care about your rules or your own safety at all?" Isadora tried tentatively, "We just wanted to support you! You know that we weren't allowed to watch the tryouts in person Cass!"

"There are smarter ways to cheer on friends that don't put you in danger!" Cassidy snapped. She took a steadying breath before continuing more calmly. "What if Broderick wasn't in such a good mood, huh? You could've been looking at detention for weeks."

I shuffled my feet. "We're sorry, we didn't think..."

"Clearly." Cassidy sighed wearily. "Look, I appreciate the thought, but no more sneaking around, okay? Promise me you'll be more careful from now on." "Yeah", Isadora replied.

After stuffing ourselves silly on snacks, we chatted happily.

Five

The days were finally counting down to reveal the official championship team rosters, posted outside the Grand Hall. Cassidy was a bundle of nerves as we waited, while I tried my best to assure her of the inevitable good news. Then, the moment arrived - students started crowding around the parchment lists eagerly. We pushed our way through and scanned the names on the parchment paper..

ASTERIA INSTITUTE SPORTS CHAMPIONSHIP SELECTIONS

FIRE MAGIC

- Amelia Lovelock
- Ethan James
- Aiden Blaze
- Keira Norton

NATURE MAGIC

- Hazel Fernandez
- Wyatt Caddell
- Rafael Torres
- Willow Oakley

WATER MAGIC

- Marina Hampton

- Kai Waters
- Neveah Greene
- Levi Stuart

LIGHT MAGIC

- Cassidy Clarke
- Angelica Browning
- Lysander Keenes
- Clara Thompson

DARK MAGIC

- Sabrina Myrtle
- Jenna Troy
- Kieran Blackwell
- Roman Vance

ICE MAGIC

- Finn Harper
- Jack Frost
- Olivia Blizzard
- Gabriel Hail

"There it is!" I squealed excitedly, pointing at the name towards the bottom of the Light Magic section. "Cassidy Clarke!"

Cassidy clapped both hands to her mouth, her eyes widening in shock and disbelief. "I made it?" she gasped.

"You made it!" Isadora and I both cheered, pulling Cassidy into a hug and bouncing up and down.

Cassidy broke into a dazzling smile, the nervous tension and worry evaporating from her face. "I actually made the team!" she said wonderingly.

"We knew you would!" said Isadora, beaming proudly at our friend.

Just then, Professor Broderick emerged from the crowd. "Congratulations Miss Flynn, well-earned!" he said approvingly. Cassidy beamed even brighter at the praise from one of the coaches.

"This calls for a celebration," I declared. "Last one back to the dormitory has to do all our Charms homework this week!"

With that, the three of us took off at a sprint, giggling madly all the way back to Light Division Tower. Once inside, we bounced on the beds and whooped with glee. Cassidy's hard work had paid off - she was officially part of Asteria's championship team lineup. I couldn't wait to cheer her on at the competitions this month!

Just as we finished laughing about Cassidy making the team, Headmistress Marietta's voice magically boomed through the school.

"All students report to the Great Hall now!"

We hurried down the stairs with everyone else, wondering what was up. The theories being thrown around included team captain announcements or extra practice schedules.

But when we got to the Great Hall, I stopped in my tracks. The place was totally decked out! Streamers and balloons in all the division colors, floating everywhere. Tables lined with more food than I'd ever seen. And was that...fireworks?!

"It's a huge celebration for the championship qualifiers!" I yelled. No way this was just another regular meal.

Sure enough, when we sat down Headmistress Marietta stood up holding a glass. "To our amazing athletes - congrats after working so hard. Now enjoy this feast in your honor!"

The whole hall erupted with cheers. As Cassidy, Iz and I dug in, we kept glancing at each other with big smiles.

The tables were overflowing with all kinds of tasty treats. There were gigantic platters piled high with roasted turkey, ham, and beef - the meats perfectly seasoned and crispy on the outside.

Steaming pots of mashed potatoes, stuffing, and buttered vegetables like carrots, green beans and corn dotted the tables. Big bowls of fluffy rice and fresh bread rolls were within easy reach.

For the Water and Ice students, there were seafood dishes like lobster tails, shrimp, and salmon prepared a variety of ways. Nature Magic students filled their plates with mushroom ragouts and stir fries featuring vegetables from the magic gardens.

Fruit pies, cakes, tarts and cups of ambrosia filled the empty spaces. The dessert section was overflowing with tempting treats. Towers of cupcakes iced in team colors, heart-shaped shortbread cookies, crispy brownies and fluffy rice pudding.

By the time Cassidy, Isadora and I had filled our plates, we could barely lift them! But we were determined to leave room to sample everything. It was a true feast fit for champions.

Between mouthfuls of turkey and mashed potatoes, we started discussing Cassidy's training schedule now that she made the team.

"Coach was saying practices will be twice a day, every afternoon and morning on weekends," Cassidy said. "Plus weights and conditioning three times a week."

Isadora shook her head in amazement. "You'll be shredded by competition time with that routine!"

"I bet we'll be doing a lot of laps around the pitch too," Cassidy guessed. "Gotta get my endurance up."

"We'll come to every practice to cheer you on," I assured her.

Isadora nodded. "And we can quiz you on defensive spells during your breaks."

Cassidy was shoveling cupcake into her mouth at an impressive speed. As she started replying to Isadora, her words came out garbled.

"Fanks guyth, dis id reeeeelly miff portant tho me." She swallowed hard. "I gowta be reaby fer-" Cassidy paused to chomp down some more cupcake.

Isadora raised an eyebrow, struggling not to laugh. "Um, could you please say that again?"

Cassidy took a big gulp of orange juice. "I said, thanks guys, this is really important to me! I've gotta be ready for the big tournaments."

She dove back in, managing a "Tho I'll need ya help wiff-" before cutting herself off with another messy mouthful of crumbs.

I couldn't hold it in anymore and burst out laughing at Cassidy's cake-stuffed face. She shot me a look that only made me howl harder.

After forcefully gulping down the rest, Cassidy sighed in defeat. "Alright, I'll slow down on the cupcakes from now on if I want to be taken seriously!"

After finishing our celebratory feast, we made our way back to the common room area in the Light Division tower. The late afternoon sun was still streaming through the tall windows as we sank into comfy chairs by the fireplace.

"I can't wait to tell my parents I made the team!" Cassidy said excitedly, pulling out her communication crystal. "Though the tournaments are months away."

"Plenty of time to practice up and get in top form," Isadora noted. She took out her magical sports almanac. "Let's look over past championships for strategies."

As Cassidy got distracted chatting with her family, Isadora and I poured over the records. "The Fire Division has won 6 of the last 10 times," I observed.

Isadora smirked. "But the stats show their defense has been weak on the left side. If Cassidy hones her spinning shot there..."

After we discussed with each other about the championship, we gathered our things and headed down, still buzzing with excitement. Upon arriving, the hall was filled with cheerful chatter among groups of students.

"Look, there's Beatrice and Clara from our division," I pointed out.

We brought our trays of scones and sandwiches over to join them. Beatrice congratulated Cassidy on making the team enthusiastically.

"Thanks! We were just going over some plays up in the Light Division department," Cassidy replied.

Clara's eyes lit up. "Ooh do tell! I want Light Division to smash the competition this year."

This launched us back into our spirited discussion of formations and techniques. Before we knew it, the sun was setting orange and purple outside the enchanted windows.

"Oh my stars! I lost track of time!" Isadora exclaimed. "We'd better head to the library to start our Potionology essays." After that, we headed to the library.

Weeks flew by in a blur of intensive training as Cassidy prepared tirelessly for the championships. True to our word, Isadora and I attended every Light Division practice to cheer her on.

The long-awaited opening day of the championships arrived! Isadora, Cassidy and I made our way eagerly to the stadium buzzing with anticipation. Track and field events would kick things off in fittingly exciting fashion.

I could barely contain my excitement as the opening day festivities began. "Look, there's Cass warming up with the team!" I pointed out to Iz.

Nearby, the Nature Division was stretching under Hazel's focused lead. "She'll be a tough competitor as always," I noted. Hazel was not one to underestimate.

When the parade started, Light Division marched through proudly. "Go Cass!" Iz and I cheered as she waved up with her radiant grin. After the commencement, the races were fast and furious.

In her 100m heat, Cass pulled ahead smoothly, breaking the finish line first. "Yes!" Iz and I high fived, elated for her victory. I spotted Marina also leading her Water Division teammates to success nearby. After an emotional victory lap, she came to find us breathless. "We've got to celebrate tonight," I grinned, engulfing her in a hug.

After the exhilarating events of the day, Beatrice, Angelica, Isadora, Cassidy and I made our way back to the Light Division dorm, buzzing with excitement.

"Congrats again Cass, you were amazing out there!" gushed Beatrice. Angelica nodded in agreement, giving Cassidy a playful punch on the shoulder. We all chatted late into the evening about the exciting events of the first championship day and Cassidy's victories. We all got tired and went to sleep after that, hoping the next championship day would go well.

Solaria was making her way to the courtyard after studying late in her office. Through the arch, she noticed a figure by the fountain under the rising moon.

It was Nyx, chanting an incantation with hands aglow. Foul magic seeped into the fountain's waters. When Solaria demanded what she was doing, Nyx replied with a cruel smile, "A parting gift."

With a cold laugh, Nyx dissolved into the fountain and was gone.

Six

"Wake up, you two!" Isadora's voice cut through the morning stillness, her tone urgent. "What? It's a Sunday!", I replied sleepily Her hands were shaking as she roughly shook Cassidy and I awake. "Something's wrong, really wrong!"

We groaned, blinking sleep from our eyes. "What's going on, Isadora?" I mumbled, rubbing my eyes.

Cassidy sat up, her face a mask of confusion. "Is it morning already?" she asked, her voice thick with sleep.

"It's morning, alright," Isadora replied, her voice tense. "But something's seriously off!"

After rushing to get dressed, we made our way downstairs to the Grand Hall. But the usually cheerful Hall was filled with whispered murmurs of unease.

I asked Beatrice, "Hey Bea, what happened?"

"Go to the courtyard and you'll see," Beatrice replied, her voice hushed.

Intrigued and alarmed, we hurried towards the courtyard. The moment we stepped outside, our breath caught in our throats. The once vibrant Fountain of Elysium, the heart of the academy, was shrouded in an ominous darkness.

A crowd of students and staff had gathered around the fountain, confused. We pushed our way through the crowd, our eyes locked on the darkened fountain. It looked as if someone had sucked the life out of it. A cold dread settled in the pit of my stomach as I realized the gravity of the situation.

"Oh moonlit waters!" Cassidy breathed, her voice filled with awe and fear.

"It's like something evil took over it," Cassidy murmured, her voice barely audible.

"We need to figure out what happened," I said, my voice steady despite the churning fear inside. "This can't be a coincidence."

Isadora looked around at the gathered students, her eyes wide with worry. "It's like a nightmare," she whispered. "The fountain can't just...die."

Cassidy nodded, her face pale. "Whatever happened, it's bad news for the whole academy."

Headmistress Marietta stood at the edge of the crowd, her face etched with concern. She raised her hand for silence and addressed the gathered students. "Everyone, please remain calm," she announced, her voice echoing through the courtyard. "We are investigating the cause of this disturbance. Until we understand what has happened, I urge you all to return to your dorms."

A hush fell over the crowd as we listened to the Headmistress. The fear in her voice was palpable, and it sent a shiver down our spines. As the students began to disperse, we exchanged concerned glances.

"We can't just stand here and do nothing," Isadora said, her voice filled with determination. "We have to figure out what caused this."

"I agree," Cassidy added, her eyes flashing with resolve. "We need to find out what's wrong with the fountain."

"The library might have some answers," I suggested. "We should start there."

Isadora nodded, her face grim. "But what if the answer is out there, beyond the academy's walls?"

"We can't just sit around and wait," Cassidy said, her voice firm. "We have to do something." "The library might have some answers," I suggested. "We should start there." Isadora nodded grimly at my suggestion. "The library is as good a place as any to start."

We delved into musty book after book, scanning pages by dim lamplight. Hours crept by as we read every book in the library. Giving up wasn't an option, the future of Asteria was at stake, we had to do something about it before it got worse.

After hours of searching, just as exhaustion was setting in, Isadora pulled an old leather-bound book from a high shelf.

"Guys, come look at this," she said urgently.

We gathered round as she carefully opened the fragile pages. It was a history of the Founders from earliest times.

Scanning the faded script by dim lamplight, Isadora began to read passages aloud. "It details how they originally came together in harmony...but then a rift formed between Nyx and the others over their views on humanity," she summed up.

A chill went through me at what she implied in her summary. It was clear that these early tensions led to the curse.

"This is promising - the information we need must be in here somewhere," Cassidy said eagerly.

Isadora read aloud a passage about the Founders' early cooperation. "But listen to this part," she said, peering closer.

"It says an 'unspecified tragedy awoke discord'. Nyx grew increasingly unhappy with humanity," Cassidy noted.

I frowned. "What could have happened to make her turn on them so much?"

Flipping ahead carefully, Isadora scanned more. "Ah, there's mention here of a dispute over a human village. But the details are faded."

Cassidy pondered this. "So the tensions really started after some incident involving mortals. Do you think that's when Nyx cursed the fountain in anger?"

"It must be related somehow," I replied. "We just need to find the full story buried here in the fragile pages."

Isadora nodded determinedly. "There's more history to uncover. Let's keep reading together and try to piece it all together."

We spent the long night in the library trying to decode what happened to the fountain.

"AHEM!"

I awoke sore-necked having dozed off among the archives. Cassidy and Isadora stirred too as dawn light filtered in.

Footsteps sounded; the grumpy librarian, Mrs Lockwood appeared frowning at our mess. "Explain," she demanded. Isadora started apologizing but yawned instead.

Thinking fast, Cassidy gestured to our notes. "We lost track of time studying but found a clue."

Curiosity overtook Pince's scowl as she glanced at our pages. For a moment, she said nothing.

With a sigh, "See you tidy up and get to lessons. No more all-nighters."

Relieved, we nodded and cleaned and straightened. We headed to our dorms to get dressed.

Suddenly, Headmistress Marietta's voice boomed over the loudspeaker: "Students report to the Grand Hall immediately. I have an important announcement."

Curious, we joined the gathering crowd. Marietta stood gravely on the stage. "Due to the ongoing issue with the founding fountain, I regret to inform you all athletic championships have been cancelled this term."

As the announcement echoed across the amphitheater, the students erupted into scowls and shouts.

"This is unfair!" yelled Amelia from the back rows. Her protest made others to join in the outcry.

Marietta raised her hands, calling for calm. "I understand this is upsetting. But for now, the fountain's curse takes priority. We must focus on lifting it before further disruption."

The crowd continued grumbling angrily as Marietta departed. Cassidy turned to us with a steely look. "She's right that it's the top priority now. Come on, let's continue researching - the faster we solve this, the sooner things can get back to normal."

As we made our way to the library after breakfast, we noticed idle groups of students milling about instead of heading to lessons.

"Wonder what's going on?" Isadora said. "Classes being cancelled too would really drive home how serious this has become."

Just then, Clara Martins jogged over. "You guys do not know? Headmistress Marietta just announced all academic activities are suspended until further notice."

Cassidy's brows furrowed in concern. "The effects of the curse must be worsening if it's disrupting schooling altogether now."

Isadora nodded grimly. "That just means the pressure's on us even more to solve this mystery fast. Come on, we've got to pick up where we left off in the archives."

"Come on, we've got to pick up where we left off in the archives," I repeated after her.

"Oh come on!" Isadora groaned in frustration. "We've been at this the whole night with no real leads. At this rate the whole school could just be cursed by tomorrow!"

I frowned. "Giving up won't solve anything. We just have to keep searching and hope the missing pieces will fall into place."

Seven

I was browsing the library shelves when suddenly the pieces clicked into place. My dreams, the history books, the curse—it all made sense now.

Rushing over to Cassidy and Isadora, I was practically buzzing with excitement. "Guys, I just found the answer about the curse!"

They looked up expectantly as I caught my breath. "The week before, I had a dream of Solaria and Nyx arguing near the fountain. I think I know what actually happened."

Isadora nodded, waiting for me to continue. "We're all ears, Lys." "Nyx was grieving over all the witches lost in Salem", I explained. "When Solaria said humans and magical beings could live in peace, it sent Nyx over the edge. A duel started..."

Cassidy caught on quickly. "And in her fit of anger and pain, Nyx cursed the fountain so that it would be cursed sometime in the future to force her academy to turn to her views!"

"Exactly!" I replied eagerly. "Her lingering grief and anger is what's sustained the curse all this time."

As Cassidy, Isadora and I sat discussing my dreams, I realized something important was missing. "There needs to be a cure," I said determinedly.

A thought suddenly occurred to me. "I remember reading in a book that Asteria recorded all of Solaria's magical discoveries and research."

Cassidy raised an eyebrow. "And you think...?"

"If Solaria was trying to find a way to lift Nyx's curse back then, her notes may have clues!" I said excitedly.

Isadora agreed. "It's worth a shot to check the castle. Solaria's notes could be there undisturbed all this time."

I nodded eagerly. "Solaria's archives could be there untouched for centuries. It's worth a look, don't you think?"

"It's the best lead we have so far," Cassidy agreed.

After debating logistics, we decided to sneak away that weekend to search the abandoned castle ruins ourselves. ANYTHING to help break this curse and get our lives back to normal.

We started in the west wing, close to where we had our classes. The empty corridors felt almost haunted in the evening stillness. I couldn't help peering into dark classrooms as we passed.

"Anything interesting?" Cassidy asked. I shook my head. Nothing but dusty desks and boards staring back.

Isadora noticed a narrow stairway leading upwards between the alchemy and charms sections. "Let's check the restricted area." Dust motes danced in the beams as we climbed into obscure volumes locked away for centuries.

Our search continued across campus - the conservatory was a maze of twisted trees and strangling vines. The potions lab held suspicious stains and lingering scents that made us shudder. In the astronomy tower, I peered through an enchanted star-chart and felt briefly dizzy as constellations whirled. But still we found nothing useful regarding the curse.

As dusk fell, our search had turned up nothing in the ruins.

"There's still one place we haven't checked," I said hesitantly.

Cassidy eyed me warily. "You don't mean...the old North Hall, do you?"

Isadora gulped. "After what happened to Josephine?"

I steeled my nerves. "Rumor is Solaria's hidden archives may be sealed in the lowest levels. It's said to be haunted but...what if that's where the solution to the curse is hidden?" We started to exchange uneasy glances, but after a while, they finally nodded. "You're right, we have to try everywhere". As the door opened with a shriek, wispy figures coalesced before us.

The ghosts appeared before us, no longer frightening.

"Greetings. We mean you no harm," one said.

Cassidy stepped forward. "Thank you for not scaring us. We're trying to lift Nyx's curse and save our school. Can you tell us anything that might help?"

"Hmm, well Solaria used to carry a special book of her spells," the ghost replied thoughtfully. "A grimoire, I believe she called it. Contained counters and spells for all her discoveries, if memory serves."

Isadora spoke up. "Do you know what happened to it after she...you know."

The ghost shook its head. "Alas no, just stories it held great power. But logically, Solaria would want to defeat the curse straight away."

I nodded. "So maybe the grimoire with the counter-curse is here somewhere, hidden all this time!"

"Worth a look around," Cassidy agreed. "Thanks for your help, spirits. We won't touch anything else."

After leaving the ancient ruins, we settled at a corner of the library and started to discuss the lost grimoire. Cassidy leaned forward, her eyes wide with curiosity. "So, Solaria's grimoire could be the key to lifting the curse?" I nodded, "That's what the ghosts in the ruins said. Solaria carried it everywhere, and it contains all her original spells." Isadora tapped her chin thoughtfully. "If it's that important, it's likely hidden somewhere secure. We need to figure out where she might have kept it." Cassidy pulled out a notepad. "Let's list possible places. Solaria had her private quarters, right? Maybe she kept it there."

Lysandra shook her head. "Her quarters were searched long ago. It wasn't there. The grimoire might have been hidden somewhere else—somewhere only she would know."

Isadora's eyes lit up. "What if she used a secret passage or enchanted vault? We've seen old blueprints of the castle that mention hidden rooms. We should check those." Cassidy yawned, "I don't know about you guys, but I'm getting really sleepy, I'm heading back to sleep." "Yeah, me too, let's head back to our dorms", Isadora said.

After that, we started to head back to our dorms for some sleep.

"I can barely keep my eyes open," Cassidy yawned.

Just then, we heard giggling from behind a broken wall. Amelia Lovelock popped out, smirking.

"Well, well, what do we have here? Sneaking out after hours again, Lysandra?" she mocked.

I sighed inwardly, preparing for Amelia's usual jabs. But tonight, I was too tired to rise to the bait.

"Mind your business, Amelia," I replied curtly, attempting to walk on.

But she darted ahead, blocking our path with a coy smile. "Ooh, somebody's touchy! What were you really up to out here, hmm?"

Her eyes glinted mischievously as she glanced between us, clearly fishing for gossip. Behind her back, Cassidy rolled her eyes.

"Nothing that concerns you," I said bluntly, avoiding eye contact. "Now move along, please."

Amelia pouted, but finally complied with an irritating giggle. "Alright, keep your secrets. But I'll find out what you're hiding eventually..." I ignored Amelia. We started to head back to sleep, hoping that we would find clues tomorrow.

Eight

The next morning, we made our way to Solaria's old headquarters in the Light Magic Department, in hopes of finding the answer. Dusty old books held no insights to the curse anyway. When we arrived, we started exploring. The old headquarters was in a run-down state after years of neglect. Torn tapestries on the stone walls showed pictures of Solaria and students, frozen in time. Shelves lined the curved back wall but were long empty. A few remnants of old potion bottles and worn books remained.

As we looked around the dim headquarters, I gazed up at the tapestry of Solaria and her students. "They all seem so determined, like they were working on something big," I said.

Cassidy nodded as she brushed dust off a shelf. "Well we're carrying on their mission now in a way, trying to lift the curse off the fountain."

Isadora was flipping through a ragged book nearby. "Guys, come look at this! It mentions magical artifacts Solaria was studying." We gathered round as she pointed out phrases on disintegrating pages.

Although much of the text was lost, it described Solaria's interest in ancient relics said to hold mystifying powers. "Maybe she hid something here for safekeeping," Cassidy suggested.

We spread out searching the shadowy chamber more attentively. Behind a gap in the wall, I found skeletal remains of bookshelves. Rummaging the dust, my fingers closed around a glass vial stopped with wax. But no grimoire appeared yet.

"Well, well. The little researchers are at it again I see." She sauntered over, peering over our shoulders. "Any dark secrets or scandals in these moldy pages?" As we poured over another dusty tome, faint footsteps echoed behind us. I turned to see Amelia leaning against the doorframe, smirk in place.

I snapped the book shut. "What do you want, Amelia?" Her constant intrusions were the LAST thing we needed.

But she only grinned more. "Oooh, a girl can't check in on her classmates? I'm interested in what you're up to." Her eyes glinted with mischief. "Or should I say, who?"

Cassidy scowled. "We're trying to solve an ancient curse. But I'm sure petty gossip is more your speed."

Amelia feigned offense. "No need to get testy! I was just offering my help." She waved her wand, sending a puff of dust our way. "Ta for now."

Cassidy closed the old book she was looking through. "You know, I'm not finding much in here and my stomach is growling."

Isadora nodded. "Yeah, we've been at this for a while. A break would be good."

I stretched my back which was sore from bending over so long. "Any ideas where to look next after lunch?"

Cassidy stood up. "No clue yet. But maybe some food will help us think of new places to search What do you say we grab a bite in the Grand Hall before tackling this again?"

"Sure, I could eat," I agreed. The rumbling in my stomach was a reminder I'd skipped breakfast focused on our search for clues.

Isadora slipped the last book back on the shelf. "Sounds good."

We headed to the Grand Hall for some food. We had just started eating when Professor Priestley came striding over. "Girls, Amelia said she saw you all sneaking into the abandoned wing earlier. You know that area is off limits."

Isadora looked confused. "But we had permission from Headmistress Marietta to research there."

Priestley's brow furrowed. "The headmistress didn't inform me. What exactly were you looking for?"

Before I could answer, Cassidy spoke up angrily. "We weren't sneaking around, Amelia's lying. She just wants to cause trouble as usual."

The professor sighed. "I'll have to verify what you said with Headmistress Marietta. In the meantime, I suggest choosing your activities more carefully to avoid these situations."

As she walked off, Cassidy scowled. "Ugh, I bet Amelia isn't even in real trouble. She just loves messing with us."

Our mood was ruined by the encounter. As we were about to leave the Grand Hall, Headmistress Marietta was there speaking to Professor Hawthorn.

"I assure you I didn't give anyone permission to be in the abandoned wing," Marietta said, brow furrowed in confusion.

Hawthorn turned towards us. "Girls, the headmistress claims she knows nothing about your supposed activities there. Care to explain?"

I felt a rush of anger at Amelia for painting us in an even worse light. "We must have misunderstood, but Amelia's clearly lying about catching us there," I said firmly.

"How about you three come to my office?" Marietta said, in a stern tone. We exchanged worried faces, knowing we were in trouble. Then, we started heading to her office. Headmistress Marietta sat behind her desk as we entered.

"Thank you for coming. I've spoken to Amelia and the truth is clear." Marietta sighed. "While I understand your research, sneaking into forbidden areas causes problems."

"We weren't sneaking, we just misunderstood the rules," Cassidy replied.

Marietta held up a hand. "Regardless, it gave opportunity for mischief. In the future, come directly to me with such inquiries. Is that understood?"

We all nodded. There wasn't much else to say since she was right.

As we walked away from Marietta's office, Cassidy scoffed. "I can't believe Amelia put us through all that trouble just to cause drama."

Isadora nodded. "She really has it out for us. I wish there was a way to get her off our backs."

"Don't let her bother you," I told them. "We'll figure this out despite her attempts to sabotage us."

As we made our way back inside to our dorms to rest, I noticed Isadora was quietly crying.

"What's wrong?" Cassidy asked with concern.

Isadora sniffed. "I-I'm just feeling so discouraged. We've looked everywhere and still have no real answers. What if we never solve this? The curse will remain forever!"

I put an arm around her shoulders. "Don't lose hope yet. We knew this wasn't going to be easy. And we've only just begun investigating new spots today."

"Yeah, there're still so many places we haven't tried," Cassidy added. "The library has loads more books too. And who knows what Headmistress Marietta may know to help."

Isadora took a shaky breath. "You're right. I'm letting my frustration get the better of me. We have to keep going, for Solaria and the school."

"We're in this together," I assured her. "Now come on, let's hang out!"

Isadora suggested playing a game of Snakes and Ladders.

We arranged ourselves around the board as she explained the familiar rules. Reaching the end required luck in landing on ladders or avoiding deadly snakes.

I rolled first, landing on a space that triggered a gleeful song from the board. As the ladder's magic lifted my piece, Cassidy jokingly grasped at empty air in faux terror.

When her turn came, Cassidy's hopes crashed as a snake's jaws snapped shut behind her token. "Not fair, these magical modules never work in my favor!"

Isadora simply smirked as her first few rolls granted swift climbs up ladders. But karma struck when a mischievous rune twisted her piece backwards.

Growing bold in my lead, I taunted my friends by blocking their attempts to pass me. Isadora retaliated by enchanting my dice to only roll ones for the rest of the game.

As we we were hanging out, Cassidy opened her Beginner's Book of Spells. Many charms we had studied, but some were still mysteries. She asked us to be test subjects for a softening enchantment meant to supple leather. Isadora volunteered. Cassidy performed the spell and Isadora's boot instantly felt like a soft slipper! It was so funny! After that, we started to wrap up our day by going to sleep.

Nine

The next morning, my eyes fluttered open feeling unusually restless. There was a nagging sensation pulling me back to Solaria's old headquarters like an invisible thread. Rolling over, I saw Cassidy and Isadora still dozing in the predawn light. I didn't want to disturb them if it was nothing. But as I lay there contemplating, the pull only intensified.

Quietly climbing out of bed, I got dressed while mulling over the strange urge. It wasn't like any normal hunch - this felt deeper, like someone was quietly urging me to return. The more I considered it, the stronger the conviction grew in my gut.

Once dressed, I gently nudged Cassidy's shoulder. "Cass, wake up. I think we need to check the ruins again," I whispered. Her eyes blinked open groggily.

"What, whyy?, what is it?" she yawned, rubbing the sleep from her eyes. As I explained the peculiar feeling drawing me back, alertness returned to her face.

We roused Isadora next, who looked at me skeptically until I insisted. "I can't explain it fully, but I really believe we'll find something if we go now," I pressed.

Both my friends saw the sincerity in my face and reluctantly agreed. Quickly getting ready in the dim light, we hurried off-grounds before dawn fully broke over the hills.

We headed straight to the hidden chamber, taking our time to examine every nook and cranny more closely than before. I ran my hand along the rough stone wall, peering intently for any signs we may have missed. Isadora swept away more layers of dust and debris with magic, while Cassidy focused on the walls and floors.

I was about ready to admit defeat when Cassidy called out excitedly. "Come look at this, I found something!" We hurried over to where she was crouched by the edge of the wall. "Feel along here, there's something odd about these grooves."

Isadora and I joined her, tracing our fingers over the ridges and dents in the stone. They did seem too uniform and patterned to be natural. "Can you shift that section at all?" I asked Cassidy.

She wedged her fingertips into two tight indentations and leaned her weight forward. With a grinding scrape, a small section of the wall popped loose, revealing the opening of a hidden chamber beyond. Dust billowed out as we coughed, waving it away to peer inside. An eerie blue glow emanated from within the small space.

Entering the newly revealed chamber, we shone our wands around the small dusty space. At first, it seemed empty aside from cobwebs. And then, Cassidy gasped.

"Look at this on the floor, is that...parchment?" she said in a hushed voice.

We hurried over and saw a tattered square of cream-colored paper partially rolled up. I carefully lifted the corner, but the page was completely blank despite an odd shimmer.

"Do you guys feel that magic coming off it too?" Isadora asked softly. We all nodded, exchanging puzzled looks. Somehow we sensed this was no ordinary find.

As I peered at the parchment paper, an idea struck me. "What if we spoke to Headmistress Marietta about this?"

Isadora shifted nervously. "I don't know, after the trouble Amelia caused yesterday..."

"Marietta wants us to come directly to her with our research, remember?" Cassidy added supportively.

I turned to Isadora. "I know you're worried, but Marietta has been trying to help. She might know what this means."

Isadora frowned, gazing between us unsure. Then with a sigh said, "You're right. Anything to move our search forward."

Relief swept through me taking her hand. "We'll do it together so she sees we're being honest."

Hurrying back to campus, we started to head to her office.

As we knocked on Marietta's door, Isadora hung back nervously.

"What if she thinks we were sneaking around again?" Isadora whispered anxiously.

I took her hand reassuringly. "Marietta will understand we were just researching. This could help us SO MUCH to lift the curse!"

"But what if she takes the parchment away and we never see it?" Isadora worried.

Cassidy chimed in. "We won't know unless we try. And we can tell her we don't want it out of our possession."

Isadora still seemed uncertain as Marietta called us in. She lingered by the door as Cassidy and I launched into our explanation.

Only when Marietta asked sharply where we'd found it did Isadora speak up hesitantly. "Well...in a hidden chamber. But we didn't mean to cause trouble, we just want to help."

Marietta fixed her sharp gaze on Isadora. "I understand your concern, my dear. But this artifact is crucial to solving many mysteries. You have my word I will not seize it from your care without consent."

As Isadora watched on nervously, Marietta took it gently. "This is an heirloom passed through Solaria's lineage. But how did you come to possess it?"

I explained how we found the hidden chamber. Marietta nodded thoughtfully as she listened.

"Its protective magic lasted well. But the right incantation can reveal the contents of the paper." She retrieved some supplies from her cabinet - candles, crystals, an ornate key.

Pricking her finger, Marietta let a drop of blood fall on the page. Then she began chanting in an ancient language, motions flowing as power swirled visibly. Her spell gained intensity with hand movements and a final cry.

For a moment, nothing. Then slowly, words bled through the vellum like spilling ink, spreading names and illuminating a vast tree. The parchment paper then appeared, with Solaria's lineage! It was so fascinating! We leaned in to get a better look at the family tree. Isadora pointed out famous descendants we had learned about. I noted similarities in spellwork passed down through generations.

Moving ahead through the centuries, Marietta paused on a familiar name. "Here is Solaria herself, founding your school so so long ago!" We pictured the proud fairy in her painted likeness.

Marietta smiled. "Fascinating history here." My hand froze when I spotted a name.

"Hold it up, did that say..." I trailed off, re-reading in disbelief. Cassidy and Isadora crowded in for a look..

Nobody said anything for a minute. I just stared at the name, my brain trying to process. Finally Cassidy broke the silence.

"No way, you're actually related to Solaria??"

Isadora squeezed my arm. "I knew something was guiding you back there!"

Marietta's eyes lit up. "Fate works in strange ways. You were meant to find the answers, Lysandra."

My mind was blown. Related to Solaria? Inheriting her magic? It was nuts. But Marietta reassured me with a smile.

"Don't stress about it all now. The meaning will become clear over time." Her words calmed my thoughts.

Cassidy threw an arm around me, beaming. "This is awesome! No wonder you were having visions of Solaria and Nyx!" Isadora nodded eagerly. "I still can't believe you're actually descended from Solaria," Cassidy said in wonder.

I was still processing it myself. "It does explain a few things...", I added.

The rest of that day passed in a joyful daze. We three could barely contain our excitement over my discovery! As evening fell, we sneakily packed supplies and snuck away into the forest beyond the school grounds.

"Can you believe Lysandra actually has Solaria's magic flowing in her?" Cassidy whispered in awe for what felt like the hundredth time. Isadora grinned. "And to think, she's the one who's going to break the old curse!"

We cast muffling charms around our little clearing and eagerly began unpacking the feast we had swiped from the kitchens.

Cassidy pulled out warm pumpkin bread and an assortment of jams. Isadora produced toasted nuts, dried fruits and slabs of creamy goat cheese. I added flaky pastries stuffed with savory mushrooms and herbs.

As we gorged on the delicious snacks, barely taking time to chew in our excitement, Cassidy started reenacting Solaria using dramatic hand gestures. "And with a wave of her hand, the evil warlock was struck down!"

Ten

The next morning, Professor Priestley pulled us aside. "Girls, the Headmistress would like a word about Solaria's private workshop."

We exchanged excited glances and hurried to Marietta's office. "I understand you've had some insightful visions, Lysandra. And given your lineage, there may be more to discover in Solaria's workshop." She handed me an ornate key. "This unlocks the wards she placed. Go see what you can find." After talking to the Headmistress, we started to make our way to Solaria's old workshop, hoping that we would be able to discover something. Stepping inside the workshop, we fanned out looking at everything with wonder. "Look at these intricate star charts!" Isadora said. I studied Solaria's crowded chalkboards. "Her mind must have worked so fast, jumping between theories."

Cassidy was flipping through a massive tome. "This details all her spell formulas - so organized!"

As the morning light shifted, Cassidy's stomach growled loudly. "I think it's time for a lunch break!"

Isadora laughed. "Agreed, we can't think on empty stomachs."

I smiled. "The Grand Hall always have leftovers we can nab. Let's go refuel then come back with fresh eyes."

Over generous sandwiches and tea in the courtyard, we discussed strategy.

"I bet it's hidden somewhere clever, like behind a bookshelf," Cassidy mused.

Isadora tilted her head thoughtfully. "What if it's in the rafters somehow? She did have quite a few telescopic charms up there."

I frowned. "It needs to be somewhere only her kin could access. But where would resonate with her bloodline?"

Cassidy suddenly straightened. "What about that weird spiraling rune on the workshop door? I'll wager it's some kind of lock."

Isadora nodded eagerly. "Ooh good catch! I didn't notice that before."

I rubbed my chin. "Only way to know is by examining it closely. Maybe my magic will recognize what it needs." Finishing our lunch, we made our way back to the workshop.

Back in the workshop, I stepped up to examine the strange swirled symbol on the door more closely. As I traced it, I felt a spark of familiar warmth.

"This seems magical, not just decorative." My friends crowded next to me. "But what's it unlocking?" Cassidy whispered.

Squinting, I noticed the subtle indent of a handprint within the spiral grooves. "It's a lock, one that responds to bloodline!"

Cassidy gasped. "Only her kin could access what's beyond. Do you think..." Isadora trailed off eagerly.

Heart racing, I pressed my palm to the lock. For a moment, nothing, then a gentle heat emanated from where our skins met. The symbol flashed brightly before receding into the door!

A hollow thump signaled something unlocking behind. Exchanging excited grins, I slowly pulled the door open to reveal a secret small room. And resting upon a worn stone table within...was the leather-bound grimoire! WE COULDN'T BELIEVE OUR EYES! Resting upon the worn stone table was a large, ornately bound leather book - the color and texture of the cover were VERY well preserved despite its old age. Intricate circular patterns were tooled into the leather, and an glowing orange gem was set into the center of each circle.

When I reached out to touch it, the gems began to pulse with light in sequence, traveling from one to the next as if responding to my presence. "It's recognizing you - it must be responding to your bloodline," Cassidy said in quiet amazement.

"I think this is what we've been searching for all along! Come on guys, let's head over to the Headmistress's office to report to her about our huge discovery!" Clasping the grimoire in our hands, we started to head to the Headmistress's office. We could barely contain our excitement at what this discovery could mean for our school AND future!!

We burst into Marietta's office and announced, "WE'VE FOUND IT! Solaria's lost grimoire!"

The Headmistress looked up in astonishment from her paperwork. "You located her private book of spells? But how?"

We started explaining everything to the Headmistress.

"This is great news for our school! The curse has plagued us for too long," said Headmistress Marietta, her eyes shining with unshed tears of joy and relief.

She held out her hands. "May I see the grimoire? As director of the academy, it is my duty to lift this curse once and for all." I gently handed the grimoire to the headmistress. I couldn't believe it when Headmistress Marietta found the counter-curse. She let out a laugh and said Solaria had left us the answer all along.

All those careful spells in her grimoire were gonna lift the curse for good, if we did it right with the moon. I was so relieved! Cassidy and Isadora smiled at me, happy it all worked out.

Marietta thanked me for finding the book. She said now we could prep to break this dark magic once and for all. The whole school started cheering that we'd finally be free.

I still couldn't believe my great-great ancestor had left us the way to save our school after all these years. Her grimoire let me finish what she started. Our curse was gonna be over for real this time!

Eleven

That night, Headmistress Marietta threw a huge celebration in the Grand Hall to celebrate. There were colorful lights shining everywhere and delicious food piled high.

She gathered us in front of everyone and said "Without these three brave Light Magic fairies, we never would've discovered the key to lifting our curse. Please join me in thanking Lysandra, Cassidy, and Isadora!"

The whole school clapped and cheered loudly for us. I couldn't stop smiling as Marietta placed medals around our necks for "Heroes of the Academy." Cassidy and Isadora high-fived me, beaming.

After her speech, music started playing and everyone danced and laughed in the moonlight. It finally felt like a weight was off all our shoulders. No more worrying about failing tests or the evil magic trapping us here. As the celebration raged on, Amelia stood alone in the shadows, glaring daggers at us three. Her hands curled into fists as she overheard another student say, "That's Amazing! They're sure to go down in history for this." Now was the time to perform the counter-curse on the fountain.

Marietta stood atop the stone ledge, grimoire open in hand. With the assistance of several elder teachers, she began to chant the complex incantation. Their voices rose and fell in an intricate magical rhythm.

Runes floated from the Headmistress's outstretched palms, sinking into the crystal waters. As they spoke the final verses, a glow emanated from within the fountain's center.

The teachers joined hands, channeling their combined power into its depths. Slowly, darkness peeled away like dead leaves, revealing a vibrant light from long ago. A brilliant flash burst from the waters, rippling outward in shimmering waves! The fountain was now free of the curse!

That night, the headmistress also announced that the Sports Championships that were canceled under the curse will now be reopened. Cassidy was very excited after she said that! By the next morning, the news of the counter-curse and championships being reopened spreads like WILDFIRE across the school. For Cassidy and her teammates, it was the opportunity they had long dreamed of! Their usual training sessions took on new intensity. Every free moment was spent running drills, practicing plays, and improving their skills.

Cassidy threw herself into extra flying and agility work, determined to strengthen her assets. She often stayed late into the evening, circling the pitch under moonlight. Isadora and I did our best to keep her fueled with hearty post-practice meals. Between training sessions, Cassidy, Isadora and I often caught our breath by the courtyard fountain. On one such afternoon, we spot Amelia marching over with her usual entourage.

"Still working yourselves to the bone I see," she sneered. "As if all that effort will amount to anything against the true champions, the Fire Magic athletes!"

Cassidy wiped her brow. "Jealous that Light's skills have surpassed yours, Amelia? We'll wipe the floor at Championships."

Amelia laughed mirthlessly. "Doubtful. I've been training twice as hard as you pathetic idiots. My team moves like lightning while yours struggle through drills!"

Isadora rolled her eyes. "Keep talking trash Amelia." As we were leaving the Grand Hall after lunch one day, a group of students from our division approached us nervously, "We wanted to warn you, Amelia's been going around saying terrible things about you guys," one of them said quietly.

Cassidy frowned. "What kind of things?"

"She told everyone you've been cheating on drills, using magic to enhance your skills illegally," another piped up.

Isadora rolled her eyes. "Classic Amelia, can't accept someone might actually be better than her."

I asked the fairies how widely it was spread. One shrugged helplessly. "Pretty much the whole school by now I think, except for the Light Magic division".

Cassidy balled her fists, trying to walk to the Fire Dorms to confront Amelia. We held her back.

"Hey! Don't listen to those rumors," one fairy said. "We know you'd never cheat. You're the best flyers here!"

Her words made Cassidy feel better as we headed to training with her. There, our classmates greeted us with pats on the back and words of encouragement.

"Who cares what Fire division gossips?" I said. "Their jealousy means nothing out on the field."

Professor Broderick gives us an appraising nod. "Keep your noses clean and let your talent do the talking where it counts. Now run the obstacle course, I want to see improvement!"

His faith bolstered us as we pushed into another grueling session. In classes, Light students stuck by our sides, drowning out Amelia's dissenters with cheers for our team. The days counted down swiftly until the re-opening of the Championships. As the long-awaited event drew near, excitement permeated every inch of the school.

In classes, it became a struggle to focus on lectures as we chatted animatedly about predictions for our divisions.

Cassidy and her teammates trained with a laser focus, honing every last detail.

The day before the opening swimming match, we decided to relax by the lake to calm our nerves. As we ate, our discussion turned to last-minute tactics.

Cassidy was demonstrating an underwater maneuver when suddenly she let out a yelp. "Lysandra, I think your wand hand is twitchy from nerves! "

Confused, I look over to see her thrashing wildly in the water, sandwich floating away.

It took me a second to realize it - my wand hand must've flicked unconsciously during my charades, casting a minor Jinx! I was overcome by giggles at the sight of Cassidy now spinning in circles helplessly.

"Lysz call itz offff!!!" she pleaded dizzy. Zipping shut my laughter, I swiftly chanted the counter-spell. Cassidy stopped spinning, gasping for breath with a groan.

"Some swimmer you'd make like that tomorrow," I teased, helping her ashore. She glowered half-heartedly as I apologized for the accidental magic mishap.

Twelve

The next day finally arrived, the opening ceremony and the first matches kicked off the revived Sports Championships!

Cassidy and I stood with the Light Magic team as Coach Broderick gave his pre-race pep talk. I could tell Cassidy was nervous, so I whispered encouragement like always. Nearby, Isadora grinned and flashed us a thumbs up.

"Alright, gather around! Today is the big day we've all been training for. I want to see some fire in those fins, you hear me?!"

The team huddled, buzzing with nerves and excitement. Broderick paced before them like a prowling lynx.

"What do we do?!" he bellowed.

"Win!" the team roared back.

"I can't hear you! WHAT DO WE DO?!"

"WIN!" They shouted louder, fists pumping.

"That's more like it!" Broderick boomed, slamming a massive hand on a cowering freshman's shoulder. "We've been pounding the water like freakin' Poseidon himself! Now it's time to show these flashy posers what Light Magic is made of."

He jabbed a finger at the rival divisions jeering nearby. "They think just because we don't cheat with spells we can't keep up? Prove. Them. Wrong!"

The coach's eyes gleamed fiercely. "I want you maggots swimmin' so fast they'll think you apparated! Feel the BURN and drive! It's all or NOTHIN' out there! Now who's taking home that gold medal?!" "US! LIGHT MAGIC!" they bellowed as one. As the morning progressed, swimmers from all six divisions took to the water - Light Magic, Dark Magic, Nature, Fire, Water and Ice. Isadora and I cheered on our Light Magic teammates. The judges floated nearby, scoring each race based on speed and form. Points would be awarded to the top finishers in each heat as well as the relays, adding up towards an overall divisional score.

The teams lined up at their starting blocks. A hush fell over the crowd as the judges raised their wands. At the blast of light, the first heat was underway.

From lane one, Dark Magic struck like sharks, slicing the water black as night. In two, Nature glided with the waves' rhythm. Fire in three shot flaming orange trails behind them. Water division bubbled forth in four, at home in their domain.

Beside them, Light Magic cut bright silvery wakes. And from the far lane, Ice magic melted across the surface, leaving a shimmering sheen.

Neck and neck down the first lengths, it was anyone's race. But at the turn, Dark Magic surged ahead, slapping the wall in a blur. Fire was close behind with

Nature gaining. Light Magic touched just after, cheering Cassidy along as anchor.

The next heat saw new competitors battle it out. From Water, Marina powered with the grace of a dolphin. Beside her, Finn from Ice zipped nimbly through the chill. Bolder still, Dark Magic's Sabrina muscled the water black.

But it was Water's Kai Waters who touched first.

As the final heats concluded, tension gripped the stadium as points were about to be awarded. The head judge cleared his throat:

"In first place, with a time of 2 minutes flat...Kai Waters of Water Division!" The crowd roared as Kai was lifted onto his teammates' shoulders.

The scoreboard lit up: 10 points to Water Division.

"In second place, with a time of 2:01...Cassidy Clarke of Light Division!"

The crowd roared as Light Magic earned 9 points on the board.

"And in third place, with a time of 2:04...Oakley Greene of Nature Division!"

Nature's score jumped to 8 points.

Continuing down the placing fairies: "Fourth goes to Keiran Blackwell of Dark Magic with 7 points. Fifth is Amelia Flame of Fire Division with 6.5 points."

With the top 5 swimmers named, their respective divisions racked up crucial early points on the tournament scoreboard:

Water Division - 10pts Light Division - 9pts Nature Division - 8pts Dark Magic - 7pts Fire Division - 6.5 pts Ice Division - 6pts

"Woohoo!" Cassidy cheered, pumping her fist in the air. Her teammates swarmed around her, whooping and hollering with joy.

"You were amazing out there!" I added.

"That finish was perfection!!" added Luke Martins from Light Magic, giving her a high five. The celebrations went on for a whole day. Everyone from our division were super ecstatic!

The sun rose on a new day of events - fairy gymnastics were up next. Isadora and I claimed our usual spot in the stands, armed with two big bags of contraband popcorn from the kitchens.

"Look, there's Cassidy warming up on the apparatus floor," I said to Isadora. We watched as she stretched and practiced flips.

Cassidy cartwheeled gracefully between the balance beams and vaults, rehearsing her routine. Other students from the divisions limbered around her, executing twirls and aerial maneuvers. Once the individual routines were completed, it was FINALLY time for the division championships. The judges raised their wands to get things started.

"Break a wing out there, Cassidy!" Isadora hollered excitedly. She pumped her fist in the air.

I grabbed Isadora's hand. "Ya got this, Light Magic!" I shouted at the top of my lungs. Nature Division led off with Wyatt Caddel, Hazel Fernandez and Rafael

Torres coordinating seamlessly on balance beam. Transitioning to floor, they wove in and out in a leaf-scattering dance. Dark Magic centered their vaulting on Keiran Blackwell and Sabrina's elite flips and twists. Jenna Troy anchored their floor with moody spins and leaps.

Fire relied on Amelia's gymnastic flaming kicks and aerial tumbling passes. Lindsay Ember and Xavier cinder linked acrobatic elements on beam.

Water's Marina Waters wowed on bars with tight-gripped swings. Sasha Bubble and Kai Waters' synchronized dives into their pool themed floor earned high-fives. When it was Light Magic's turn, the stadium fell silent with anticipation. Lysander and Angelica strode out confidently, launching into synchronized back walkovers across the foam flooring. Their timing and extension were FLAWLESS.

Next, Cassidy and Clara took to the balance beam with grace. Cassidy floated between mounts, gliding into aerials as the others moved seamlessly around her. They wove in and out like rays of sun through clouds.

Up fifth were Ice Magic - winter sprites Avery Frost, Olivia Blizzard and Finn Harper flowed across the equipment, leaving frosty trails. On floor, their wintry dances blended twirls and leaps like dancing snowflakes.

When the routines were finished, the stadium held their breaths as the head judge stepped forward to announce the results.

"In sixth place with 7 points, Ice Magic Division."

"In fifth place with 7.25 points, Dark Magic Division."

"In fourth place with 8 points, Water Division."

"In second place with a score of 9 points...Nature Division!"

Roars grew as he continued, "In third place with 9.5 points, Fire Division!"

All eyes locked on the top spot. A long pause built the suspense. "And your champions, with a perfect score of 10 points...Light Magic Division!"

The Light Magic team erupted with cheers! I watched Cassidy hug her teammates, beaming from ear to ear. Coach Broderick lifted her into a congratulatory spin.

Soon Light Magic's athletes all gathered before their stand. "Great work out there today, fairies," Broderick praised them. He turned to address Isadora and me.

"And thank you for your constant encouragement, Lysandra and Isadora. It fuels our division's success." We grinned bashfully at the praise.

We squealed and pulled Cassidy into a hug. "You were phenomenal as always!" Isadora and I gushed. The next competition day is Archery. At the archery grounds, divisions were warming up and tuning their wooden longbows. Isadora and I found our usual perch, snacks in hand to cheer on Cassidy.

Nature Division was up first. Wyatt steadily hit target after target from varying distances. Hazel and Willow

Oakley also found their mark with an impressive array of trick shots.

When Dark Magic took their turns, ominous storm clouds seemed to follow Keiran Blackwell's arrows. Jenna Troy and Sabrina Myrtle maintained pinpoint control too.

Fire kept things lively - Amelia let fly flaming projectiles that sizzled atop the targets. Ethan James and Aiden Blaze provided reliable backup support.

Water Division had a natural fluidity to their form. Marina Waters nested arrows inside overlapping rings with grace. Sasha Bubble and Kai Waters lent steady consistency.

Ice Magic brought chill precision. Avery Frost led their regimented approach, drilling the center each time. Finn and Olivia locked things down cold.

Finally it was Light Magic's turn. Cassidy went first, finding her calm and letting the bow sing. Lysander and Angelica chimed in solid support from the pack. The archery grounds fell still as the head judge prepared to announce scores. Isadora squeezed my hand tightly in anticipation.

"In sixth place, with a score of 7 points...Ice Magic Division."

Polite claps echoed around us. "In fifth place, 8 points to Dark Magic Division."

"Water Division places fourth today, earning 8.5 points." The cheers grew louder still.

"With 9 points in third, Fire Division!" Their flames sparked the crowd wild.

"A steady 9.5 points and second place goes to Nature Division!" Nature beamed proudly.

All eyes were trained on the scoreboard as the last name was called. In a booming voice, the judge declared, "And with a near perfect score of 10 points..., Light Magic Division!" Light Magic placed in 1st place again! We were ecstatic!

The last championship day was Wing Sprint.

The energy at the stadium was electric as the wing sprints dawned. As Isadora and I took our seats, the divisions were stretching their wings below.

"Look, there's Cassidy with Coach Broderick," I pointed out to Isadora. Light Magic ran drills, practicing takeoffs and pulls into super-speeds.

When it was time for qualifications, six fairies flew at a time. Water Division caught advantage on Marina' current-riding, while Nature zipped nimbly between the trees.

Fire athletes Amelia and Aiden burned bright, rocketing ahead early. But Ice Magic gained steadily on slicker, chillier winds. It was anyone's race at this point.

Light Magic pulled through, with Cassidy and Angelica leading the charge. Nature also advanced, along with Water and Fire in a dead heat.

Down the home stretch they all tore at top speed, magical auras blazing. But diving first with arms outstretched was Amelia, an impressively quick victor.

Crossing the line second, a hair's breadth behind, was Cassidy. The stands erupted with cheers for both champions.

"Just a moment - before we confirm the final scores for the championship." Gasps echoed around us. The scoreboard reset to the beginning of the tournament.

"After reviewing all events," the judge continued, "it seems Light Magic did indeed earn first place in both gymnastics and archery."

Those victories flashed up - 10 points for gymnastics, another perfect 10 for archery. Isadora and I gripped each other tightly, nerves on edge.

"the total points for Light Magic stand at..."

The math calculated before us all. Twenty points. A full perfect score.

As confetti filled the sky, Light Magic gathered in the center of the field, clutching their trophies high. Coach Broderick addressed them proudly, "I am so proud of you all!"

They cheered for Broderick before Cassidy stepped forward to talk to her teammates. "None of this would've been possible without each of you giving your all. Thank you so much guys!"

Cassidy and her teammates embraced in a massive group hug. Then attention turned to Isadora and I waving in our stand. "Thank you for your constant support!" Cassidy called out. "You two are the best cheerleaders a division could ask for!"

That night, the school hosted a huge feast for the athletes that won the championship. This was the best year ever.

About the Author

Kaitlyn Nguyen

Nguyễn Khánh Chi Kaitlyn, an 11-year-old student at The Dewey Schools, is passionate about creative writing, reading, drawing, and dance. Her favorite author is J.K. Rowling, and she enjoys books like the *Harry Potter series*, *A Year Without Autumn* and *Has Anyone Seen Jessica Jenkins* by Liz Kessler, and *The Absolutely True Tale of Disaster in Salem* by Rosalyn Schanzer. Nguyễn Khánh Chi dreams of becoming a lawyer to help people facing difficult legal situations. She expresses a deep love for writing, stating that it allows her to bring her imaginative stories to life and give others the pleasure of experiencing them. Despite the challenges of writing, such as uncertainty about how her work will be received and the solitude of the process, her passion for the craft drives her to continue improving. Recently, her academic achievements were recognized with a fully funded scholarship for the International Baccalaureate (IB) program at The Dewey Schools, a testament to her dedication and talent.

www.ingramcontent.com/pod-product-compliance
Lightning Source LLC
LaVergne TN
LVHW041537070526
838199LV00046B/1704